The Taming of Giants

THE *Taming* OF *Giants*

BY PATRICIA GORDON

ILLUSTRATED BY GARRY MacKENZIE

The Junior Literary Guild

AND

NEW YORK . *The Viking Press*

1950

Lithographed in the United States of America
by the Reehl Litho Company, New York, N. Y.

*To the real Apodemus
and Gordon who brought
him home from school*

The Taming of Giants

Apodemus Sylvaticus was a fine upstanding young fellow, as field mice go.

From tip to tiptoe he was upstanding—the whole inch and a half of him—and his two-inch tail was wrapped tightly round his tiny shanks as he peered downward anxiously in the first dawn light.

Was it higher?

Was it lower?

Alackaday, it was higher!

It was over his bed, his nice dry bed, now dry no longer.

It was over his store of seeds, doing it no real good.

It was one—two—three knots high on the old pine stump and almost lapping at his toes.

"Botheration on all this water!" squeaked Apodemus, and he twitched his whiskers crossly.

Water in moderation Apodemus expected, being an islander born and raised in the salt meadow. He even liked water in moderation, and he could swim as well as the next mouse. But he did *not* like a flood in his bedroom.

It had not been so bad the first time, nor even the third, but to have your slumbers damped by the rising tide six nights in a row was too much. It was *much* too much.

"I shall move," said Apodemus. "I shall move at once."

He looked down at all that water. "Or almost at once."

The tide went down and the sun came up and Apodemus inspected the damage the water had done. His bed was the soggiest hay he had ever seen. His best seeds had floated away. It was most discouraging.

"I shall move," said Apodemus. "Now."

And this time he meant it.

He moved to the right and he moved to the left. He moved up and he moved down. He also moved sideways.

On the right he met Rana the Frog, who pointed out a fine homesite right next to his own. "Private swimming pool, guaranteed never to run dry, and good neighbors if I do say so myself."

To Apodemus it looked like a puddle.

"It's too wet, thank you just the same," he said and scurried off.

On the left, a Sandpiper stopped skittering across the beach long enough to pass the time of day and invite Apodemus to move over there if he liked.

10

"But there isn't anything here except sand!" protested Apo-demus.

"What more could you want?" asked the Sandpiper.

"Well, grass of course. A few flowers would be cheerful, and maybe a tree for shade." Apodemus listed his requirements.

The Sandpiper shook his head. "There is no accounting for tastes. Sand is good enough for me." He skittered on about his business.

Apodemus moved on and up, right up to the tip of a cattail. The view was fine, but the cattail *would* sway. Apodemus liked nothing better than a nice swing—but not as a permanent residence. He thought he might get dizzy if he had to swing in his sleep.

13

He moved down, all the way down into an old burrow. Down was entirely too stuffy. After all, he told himself, a Mouse was not a Mole.

Apodemus moved sideways, but sideways was a tangle of wild roses and briars that tickled. If there was one thing he could *not* stand, besides a damp bed, it was being tickled.

"Hmmm," said Apodemus. "I must go farther afield."

So he crossed three fields. He skirted one big pond where the rushes grew thick and two small gardens where lettuces were planted in tidy rows. Then he stopped. He stood very, very still.

He had come to the Place of the Giants.

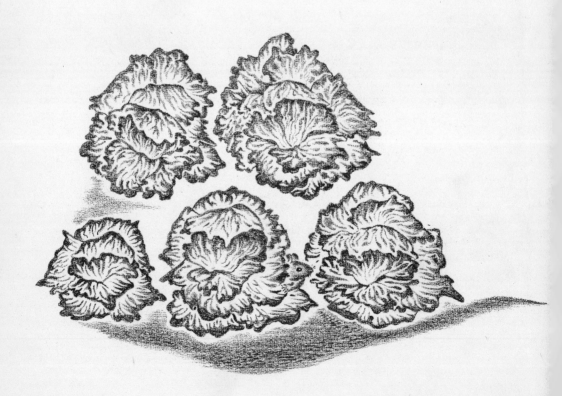

Almost a full moon ago, when Apodemus was a very young Mouse still living in the nest, his mother had brought him here. She had been explaining the dangers that beset Field Mice. She warned him about Owls, who look so clumsy and dive so fast. She warned him about Cats, with their big green eyes and sharp claws. Apodemus had shivered and promised to remember.

But Giants had to be seen to be believed.

15

So Apodemus had crouched with his mother underneath
a spray of beach plum blossom to see with his own eyes this
greatest danger of all. He had never been so frightened in
his life. The Giants were livelier than grasshoppers, and so

big he could hardly believe it. They whirled round and round
till he was dizzy and fairly deafened him with their shrieks
and howls.

Apodemus could never say he had not been warned.

Today everything was quiet, except for a steady hum inside the Giants' cave, but Apodemus knew it was perilous to linger. He was all ready to run—but his nose wouldn't let him. It twitched and it quivered, for the Most Beautiful Smell came from somewhere near the cave.

It wasn't a smell of grass or grain. It wasn't a smell of sea or flowers. It wasn't a smell he knew at all. But his nose had never failed him. If his nose said "Breakfast!" then it *was* breakfast.

His nose said, "BREAKFAST!"

Apodemus crept closer. The hum grew louder. The cave grew larger. And the Smell grew stronger.

He scurried over to the base of the cave and then began to climb. He climbed right up to the Giants' door. The door was closed, and outside it were Smells, all in a row. Apodemus darted from one to another, his nose twitching and his whiskers quivering.

The first Smell reminded him of the honey in morning-glory trumpets.

The second Smell made him think of birds for some reason. Eggs, that was it. It was like the sea-gull eggs he had found in nests in the salt meadow, only not so fishy.

The third and fourth Smells were too dull to bother about.
But the *fifth* . . .

"BREAKFAST!" said his nose.

Apodemus began to nibble.

"P-fui!" he said two seconds later.

He thought his nose had failed him for once. The Smell was beautiful, but the taste was brown and crackly.

But his nose kept right on saying "BREAKFAST!" And Apodemus remembered the store of hickory nuts his mother used to keep for special treats. Nut shells were like that, brown and crackly. You had to nibble through them to get at the delicious meats inside.

Apodemus went back to the Smell and nibbled through the brown, crackly outside, spitting out bits as he went along.

Next he came to something that made him think of seeds. The Smell had some sort of a rind as well as a shell. He chewed through and swallowed the rind, just to be rid of it.

Then he reached the Most Beautiful Smell.

His nose had been perfectly right, as always. The Most Beautiful Smell was an even More Breakfasty Taste. Apodemus wondered what it might be called.

It was so breakfasty that it tickled his nose and tickled his whiskers. Apodemus simply had to sneeze for joy.

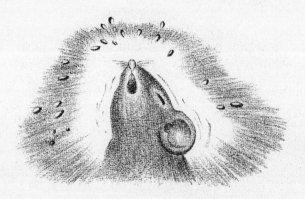

"Ah—ah—ah—*cheese!*" he sneezed.

Somehow that sounded just right. He would name it Ah-Cheese.

Apodemus nibbled straight through to the other rind. He took a deep breath and gnawed his way back again. Back and forth he went till the Ah-Cheese looked like yellow meadow rue, and his little white stomach was as tight as any cranberry in the bog.

22

At last he couldn't nibble another nibble. He couldn't gnaw another gnaw. He sighed happily and sat up to wash his face and comb his whiskers with his front paws, as any well brought up young field mouse should.

But as any well brought up young field mouse should NEVER do, he forgot to watch and listen for danger. He no longer heard the hum in the Giants' cave. He didn't hear when it changed. He didn't hear anything at all till the Giants burst out with a whoop and a roar and a shriek.

Apodemus froze where he sat, too frightened even to shiver. But a good deal was going on inside his head, and his Bump of Caution took its customary gloomy view of the situation.

"If you hadn't followed your nose," it told him severely, "you would be better off."

Apodemus was not so sure of that. It seemed to him that the situation would be worse on an empty stomach. Much worse. He thought about the Ah-Cheese, and in spite of his peril his pink tongue flickered out to see if he mightn't have overlooked just one crumb when he washed his face. He had.

"You'd have done better to stay in your nice safe home," his Bump of Caution persisted, "even if you had to swim in your sleep."

"Botheration on all this caution!" squeaked Apodemus, and he twitched his whiskers crossly. Was he Mouse or was he Minnow?

Here he was, a fine upstanding young Field Mouse. A Mouse could always make a dash for safety. Or, if he couldn't dash, he might dive—

Directly in front of Apodemus's scared black eyes loomed a dark cave. Not a Giants' cave that was almost too big to see, but a little cave just mouse-size. Head first, Apodemus Sylvaticus dived into it.

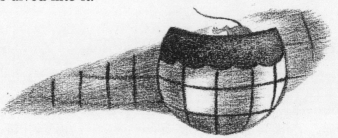

It was the most peculiar hole he had ever been in, squishy and nearly as soft as his own fur. It might even turn out to be the home he had been hunting, though it did have a few undesirable features.

It was located rather too close to the Giants for comfort, and he would have preferred it airier and with a bit of a view. But then, as his Bump of Caution was forever telling him,

24

we can't have everything. It *was* dry and cozy, and it *was* de-lightfully near the Ah-Cheese. Apodemus settled down for a nap.

He hadn't got his forty winks, nor even ten, before his new house sprang into the air, tumbling Apodemus right over on his nose.

"Ooof!" he gasped. Before he could get his balance, it happened again.

The   jumping   set
    mouse-   on   up   fairly his
       size   went   and   and   wits
       cave   down   to
                                           wambling.

To say nothing of his stomach.

27

A Nuthatch, and a very sensible fellow in spite of his name, had once told Apodemus with shudders about riding out a storm on a piece of driftwood on the Great South Bay. Seasick, the Nuthatch called it, and Apodemus decided that cave-sick was every bit as bad. He shuddered too, but that was a mistake. Cave-sick with shudders was twice as bad as cave-sick plain.

The bouncing stopped just in time to save his lovely Ah-Cheese breakfast. When the cave moved again, it was more sedately. It was rather soothing, in fact, except for a noise like a herd of Giants marching along together.

Apodemus didn't like that. Bad enough to find yourself in a cave that behaved as if it were alive, without having it move in such shocking company. But the situation improved. The cave dipped suddenly and then was still. A wonderful stillness without a solitary giantish sound to spoil it.

Apodemus had a quick think. He had to decide whether to leave now or take that interrupted nap. The way things were going, a Mouse could not be sure what might happen next, and probably he had better keep up his strength to meet it.

He wriggled down in his little cave, tucked in his paws, and curled his tail over his nose.

But, alackaday, what might happen next began to happen that very minute.

He uncurled his tail as a bright slit appeared at the top of his hole. Something pink and plump and a most peculiar wigglish shape crept in and fastened itself around him. Not until he was pulled out into the daylight could Apodemus see that a Giant's paw was holding him.

Even his Bump of Caution had no time to worry, for the paw did not hold him long. He found himself flying through the air and his ears rang with the screech that followed him.

"R-A-A-A-A-A-T-S!"

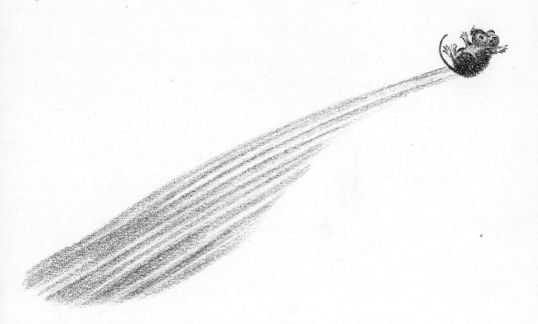

It was a pity Apodemus did not know the language of the Giants. He had once met a water rat, and he would have been enormously set up to be mistaken for such a fine big fellow.

His poor wits rattled in his head as the scream was taken up by one Giant after another. There was no doubt about it— Apodemus Sylvaticus was inside the Giants' giant cave, a fearful predicament for even the most upstanding young Field Mouse.

The Giants came all sorts and sizes. Funny-looking ones with long hair, perching on top of peculiar logs. Skinny ones jumping up and down. A fat one holding his sides. The biggest

Giant crouched over the biggest log, and his mouth kept open-
ing and shutting although no sound could be heard above the
squeaking and screeching and shouting of the others.

"R-A-A-A-A-A-T-S!"

33

It was enough to drive a mouse out of his senses. Something frightful must have scared them. Apodemus was glad he could not see what it was. If it was big enough and horrible enough to scare Giants, it was no sight for a Mouse.

He wanted to run, but something held his legs fast to the ground. Stiffening of the joints, maybe. His great-great-uncle on his mother's side got that in his old age. But it seemed too much for a young Mouse to come down with it when he needed his legs as never before.

The biggest Giant banged a round shiny thing in front of him that made a noise like the bell buoys out in the Bay, and he shouted in a voice that was a deep growl instead of a shriek.

34

It must have been the signal that the danger was past, because the littler Giants stopped screaming and sat down on their logs.

That is, all the other Giants but one, who was making straight for Apodemus, walking on its hind legs the way Giants did. Apodemus kept telling his feet to run, but that stiffening of the joints, or whatever it was, was worse than

before. Only the very tip of his nose would move at all, and that was twitching much too rapidly. A paw, skinnier and browner than the first one, closed over him.

"I hope you're satisfied," his Bump of Caution grumbled. "Now just see what you got us into."

For all the Giant's paw was so huge, it was very gentle. And this new Giant's growl was a cheerful sort of humming, something like the buzzing of Bumble Bee when he found a particularly tasty honeysuckle blossom. Slowly the paw lifted Apodemus up to a big face that was as freckled as a mackerel.

35

"Our last minute has come," said his Bump of Caution with gloomy satisfaction.

"*Will* you be quiet?" squeaked Apodemus furiously. If he had to end as Breakfast-for-a-Giant, he would meet his fate like a Mouse.

It wasn't his last minute, after all. The Giant kept on buzzing as he carried him over to one of the logs. Apodemus could not see what was going on, but he found himself dropped into another small-size cave as brown as the shell of Ah-Cheese and smelling a little bit like Ah-Cheese too. He was just wishing it was not quite so dark when the Giant pushed something bright through the sides here and there to make little windows.

"Now, that was most considerate," Apodemus told his Bump of Caution. He found that his stiffening of the joints had disappeared and he felt really remarkably well. And not nearly so much frightened as curious. That annoyed his Bump of Caution and it stopped speaking to him.

The roof of the cave opened and crumbs of seedy-smelling Ah-Cheese rind rained in on him. Apodemus thought it unfair—they didn't hurt, of course, but it was not nice to pelt him with things. Now, if it had been Ah-Cheese . . .

It *was* Ah-Cheese. The roof opened a second time and delicious snippets fell all around him. That was quite different.

"BREAKFAST!" said his nose, and Apodemus didn't say anything at all till he had swallowed the last crumb and his white fur waistcoat was a tighter fit than it had ever been before.

"Not bad!" said Apodemus as he washed his face.

"Not bad at all!" He combed his whiskers neatly.

"Just what the inner Mouse needed!" he added and yawned with full contentment.

His Bump of Caution heard him, but it didn't say a word.

Apodemus strolled across to a cave-window for a quick Mouse's-eye view of the Giants before settling down to his nap.

But Giant watching proved so fascinating that he forgot all about sleep. The biggest Giant, facing all the others over his log, would growl something in an asking sort of voice; and one after another the smaller Giants would get up on their hind legs and growl back at him.

Apodemus could even recognize the one he was beginning to think of as his Own Particular Giant. He was sure he would have known his growl from all the others, even if he couldn't see him. It was such a nice buzzy growl to listen to, except when the Giants stood up together and all the growls became singy and high, like a million mosquitoes around one pair of ears. That was terrible.

When it was over, and none too soon, the biggest Giant banged on his bell buoy. The other Giants began growling to

38

each other all at once and stowing things away. Then they got up and marched to the mouth of the cave. Apodemus's Own Particular Giant picked up the little brown cave and carried it outdoors with him.

"You see, now!" Apodemus told his Bump of Caution. "There was no need for you to take on so. He's going to let me go out here where it is safe."

His Bump of Caution was still sulking and wouldn't answer.

And it looked as if Apodemus had squeaked too soon.

Giants were bad enough, but now there was another racket, worse than all the rest and twenty times as loud. With a thumping and banging and snorting, a horrible gray Monster tore round the corner, trailing a cloud of smoke and smelling simply revolting. It had huge white staring eyes that stuck out on its head like a beetle's, and its claws were black and went round in the most peculiar fashion and so fast a Mouse couldn't really see them.

Apodemus squeaked and *squeaked* and SQUEAKED at his Own Particular Giant to run while there was time. But the Giant just stood there, holding Apodemus in his cave, and let that Monster roar right up to them. It must be that the Giant had an attack of that stiffening of the joints from which Apodemus had suffered back in the Giants' cave. Apodemus knew how he felt, and he was sorry for him. He was even sorrier for himself.

This time Apodemus *did* give up. Or his Bump of Caution did at any rate, and that was just as well. A Bump of Caution can stand only so much nervous strain in one day—and so much was quite a lot less than it had had.

Apodemus shut his eyes because he couldn't bear to see the Monster make the leap that would be the end of him and his Bump of Caution and his Own Particular Giant. He opened them again because he couldn't bear not to know when the leap was coming.

He peered through one of his windows, and then he rubbed his eyes. The Monster was standing right beside them, panting and shaking, and his Own Particular Giant was pulling out a part of it and climbing inside. This was too much. Apodemus didn't believe his eyes, so he shut them again.

A jolt shook the teeth in his head. The Monster did not like having anyone inside it, and it galloped across the sand on the beach a hundred times faster than Apodemus could run.

The little Mouse tumbled back and forth in his cave. When he was at one end, he could just catch a glimpse of white caps

and breakers. When he was at the other end, he could see bits of reeds and sky.

Apodemus didn't really care what he saw. He didn't think it mattered any more. If once you were inside a Monster, it didn't seem as if you would have much future to worry about. He almost wished his Bump of Caution would begin to scold again—it might make him feel a little less lonely.

Then the miracle happened.

Apodemus's Own Particular Giant growled. And the Monster stopped!

It stopped, shaking and panting, and Apodemus's Own Particular Giant just opened up the Monster's side again and got out, still carrying Apodemus.

You could have knocked that upstanding young Field Mouse down with a buttercup!

He wondered if it could be possible that his Own Particular Giant was brave enough and clever enough to have tamed that Monster. It must be so, for when his Giant growled again the mammoth creature hurtled on its way, without so much as snapping at them.

43

Apodemus stared out of his cave at the back of the thing. It had a flat little red tail, the only tail he had ever seen that looked sillier than a cottontail bunny's. But silly or not, and tame or not, Apodemus hardly breathed till it was a long way off.

Then he had a think.

A tamed Monster!

Hmmm. That Monster was as much bigger than his Own Particular Giant as his Giant was bigger than Apodemus—or almost, anyway. And if a Giant could tame a Monster, why couldn't Apodemus Sylvaticus tame a Giant?

45

It was a tremendous idea! It was a lovely idea!

Apodemus was thinking so hard that he didn't notice when his Own Particular Giant carried him into another cave. Then he peered out.

It was a big cave too, but nicer than the one they had left. It was his Own Particular Giant's home nest, Apodemus decided, because it had a Mother Giant in it. How Apodemus knew she was a Mother Giant he could not have told, but there was no mistaking her.

He wondered if you could tame two Giants.

He was still wondering about that when he stopped thinking to squeak with alarm. He was looking out of his own cave-window straight into a pair of eyes as big and as green as gooseberries.

"Now will you try to be so smart!" His Bump of Caution could not keep still another minute. "You and your tame Giants! These tame Giants keep a nice tame cat, and this Giant you call Own Particular brought us home to make a nice breakfast for it!"

"I don't believe it!" said Apodemus, and he twitched his whiskers crossly.

He was right, for a Giant's paw came and pushed the cat away.

Presently, after a lot of buzzy growling between the two of them, his Own Particular Giant picked up Apodemus's little cave again, and he and his Mother Giant set out with it. They walked and they walked, until Apodemus thought they must be very tired, only using their hind legs that way.

When they stopped at last, Apodemus knew even before he could see a thing that they had come to a Home Place exactly right for an upstanding young Field Mouse. It smelled just the way a home should, of grass and flowers and berries—and some Ah-Cheese.

The two Giants set his cave on the ground, and Apodemus peeked out to watch them gathering dry grass that had lots of seeds still on it. They patted it and rounded it into a very nice nest. They built a roof over it of twigs and moss and more grass to keep out the rain. Apodemus could not have done better himself.

47

When it was finished, his Own Particular Giant lifted Apodemus out of his brown traveling cave and set him down in the nest with a nice piece of Ah-Cheese to make him feel at home.

Apodemus squeaked thank you politely, and the two Giants answered him with the chuckling sort of noise that the brook made where it ran over bright pebbles. Then they got up from their knees and walked away on their hind legs.

"You can come back again any time!" Apodemus called. It would be a pity to lose a pair of Giants you had just got nicely tamed, he thought.

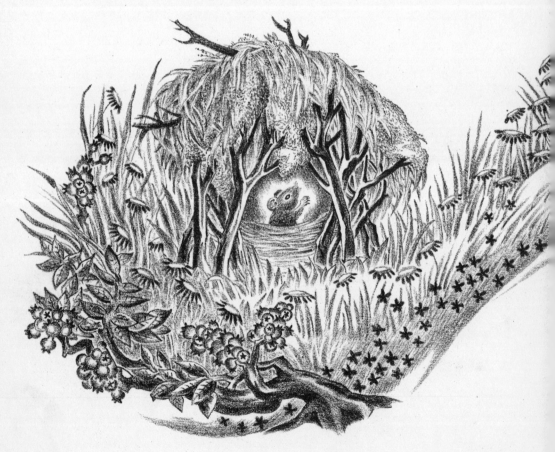

He heard that chuckling noise again.

Apodemus meant to do some exploring right away. But he was very, very sleepy. He had had a busy day and no chance to nap after any of his breakfasts. He wriggled down in his grassy nest. He tucked in his paws and curled his tail over his nose, just for a few winks.

Apodemus Sylvaticus, that fine upstanding young Field Mouse, traveler, adventurer, and Mouse of the World, was sound asleep.

The sun dropped into the sea, and one by one the stars came out, but Apodemus went on snoring softly.

Overhead an Owl circled, on the lookout for a mousy supper, but even his sharp eyes could not find Apodemus under his thatched roof. Some inquisitive fireflies saw him, but they were not ones to gossip. A Bat swooped low and saw the sleeper too, but he would never tell Owl, for he was Apodemus's own cousin Flittermouse.

Apodemus did not wake up until a morning sunbeam brushed across his eyelids.

Then he stretched and his whiskers began to twitch.

"BREAKFAST!" said his nose.

"Ah!" said Apodemus.

First things first was always the motto of Apodemus Sylvaticus. Breakfast came before exploration.

After breakfast, he was almost too full of Ah-Cheese to move, but he did manage a tour of inspection before settling down to another nap. As he thought, his new home was precisely right!

A pine tree cast dapply shadows on the soft earth and emerald grass. There was a big holly to provide juicy red berries next winter when snow would cover the ground. Apodemus was too young to have seen snow yet, but his mother had warned him to have stores on hand against the icy moontimes.

There were dewberries and blueberries for summer. He sampled them and found them almost ripe and of a fine flavor. Beach plums were already turning a rich purple if he should fancy any in the autumn.

Ladybirds in polka-dotted red coats sat upon the dandelions taking the morning air and keeping an eye on their children. And a hummingbird wearing a ruby at his throat shimmered over the honeysuckle.

And there was no more water than the bright dewdrops in holly leaf cups—just right for a Mouse to have a nice drink after his breakfast.

Even his Bump of Caution had to admit that it was not half bad, though he insisted that one never knew.

Apodemus settled down to become a social leader. All the neighbors came to call—Rana the Frog, who was quite a traveler himself; and the Red-Wing Blackbirds; and a Family of Squirrels who made cheerful company for all they were so cheeky and such teases.

His Own Particular Giant was beautifully tamed, and he came every day. And Apodemus's distant cousins became quite close relatives when they found out about the Ah-Cheese the Giant never forgot to bring.

For the sake of the Ah-Cheese they were even willing to listen politely to Apodemus's frequent and long lectures on

GIANTS AND HOW TO TAME THEM.

57